The Briar, the *Bramble,*

and the *Rose*

Shirl Knobloch

• • •

The Briar, the Bramble, and the Rose

Edited by: Jennifer Sabatelli

Cover and Artwork by: Shirl Knobloch

ISBN 13: 978-0-578-87622-1

• • •

Also By Shirl Knobloch:

Birdsong, Barks, and Banter: Adventures of an Animal Intuitive Reiki Master and Her Home of Misfit Companions

The Returning Ones: A Medium's Memoirs

You're Never Too Old for Fairy Tales

Reenactments from My Heart: Spiritual and Supernatural Civil War Fiction and Poetry

Once Upon a Fairy Tale

Strength of a Lion, Soul of a Lamb: A Collection of Wolfhound Fairy Tales and Poetry

My Ten Legged Journey: The Road to Rainbow Bridge

Waiting for the Next Village Attack: Growing Up Italian, a Jersey Girl Reminisces

Enchanted: Fairy Tales for Old and Young

• • •

The Voice of Their Hearts: Learning Animal Communication

Remembering the Magick: Fairy Tales for Those Lost, Found,
or Wandering

By Salt Water: Tales of the Sea

Spirit Whispers: A Collection of Ghostly Fairy Tales

Yes, I Knit Blankets for Squirrels: A Fairy Tale Author and Her
Bushy-Tailed Friends

Not All Witches Are Cruel, Not All Fairy Princesses Are Kind:
A Collection of Witch Fairy Tales

Being Different: A Guide for Young Empathic Mediums

Lore from Lavender Lane: Woodland Fairy Tales

● ● ●

Dedicated to Rosalie Keiko,

the prettiest Rose of all...

• • •

• • •

Table of Contents

• • •

• • •

❧ Prologue ❧

How I wish I could have been allowed to love a dog and cat as a child. That is a wish I will never outgrow. I have made up for it big time as an adult, but that child longing for all those missing years of love will never leave my soul. Those longings form who you become as an adult.

Perhaps that is why my path was always lined with waiting paws and fairy tales filled with magickal beings with fur and feathers.

❧ A Sprinkling of Stars ❧

Once upon a time, millenniums past, there shone two stars in the night sky.

"I will love you forever," said one to the other star, beaming brilliantly in the darkness.

"I am an old star," the other answered. "My forevers are coming to an end. One night, I shall set upon my final journey."

"Then I will come with you," the other star answered.

"No, your light will last longer, as it should."

No more was said on the subject, and the two stars stood quietly in the sky, looking down upon the earth. Then, the sun rose; it was time for the stars to fall asleep.

All day, the old star remained untouched by sleep, thinking of his coming journey. His light shone brighter and brighter as he thought of his dear friend in the sky, sleeping soundly next to him.

Come sunset, the younger star awoke to find his friend glimmering with intense light.

"I must look my best; my journey awaits," he whispered.

"Don't go. Please don't leave me!" the younger star cried with teardrops of light drifting, forming dozens of tiny baby stars in the sky.

"One night, long ago, I cried over another's journey, and that is how you were born in the sky. Now, it is my time, dear friend." And with that, the older star fell quickly in a blinding flash of light to the darkness below.

He fell toward a patch of field where a flock of birds slept. They were blackbirds, and the star's landing woke them all, causing them to chatter loudly in the night. A glow of light filled the sky and covered the birds.

When early morning came, the birds looked upon each other to see a sprinkling of white stars covering their feathers. They rose in flight to the heavens and flew high to the younger star, so filled with loneliness. The starlings surrounded the grieving star, the still risen moon shining on their twinkling feathers. Through their chatter, the younger star heard a familiar voice.

"My journey in the skies has not ended; it has just begun."

With that, the flock of starlings formed a wondrous murmuration in the sky. The younger star closed his eyes and went to sleep, his heart soothed by a visit from his friend.

And that is how starlings got their stars. This much-maligned bird, hated as a pest by so many and thought not worthy of a place among nature's songbirds. These beautiful birds carry falling stars upon their wings. Those who choose to see them as the wondrous beings they are will see the stars. And those who choose to listen to their ceaseless chatter will hear the words they speak and the wonderful stories they tell of stars in the sky.

Written in tribute to my own Sneezy, a rescued starling I raised from a baby. It took months for her to get her stars, as starlings are born without them. I thought of every beautiful gemstone and constellation name for her, but she had a bad respiratory infection when I found her and sneezed constantly. Every time she sneezed, I would call her Sneezy. No other name seemed to fit after that. Now, she no longer sneezes, but she will always be "Sneezy" to me.

❧ Where Love Goes ❧

Once upon a time, on an island of rolling moors and chalky cliffs, a little hare named Percy lived. He had five brothers and three sisters, but none was like Percy. Percy was a special hare, although some might call him strange. You see, Percy talked to the wind.

From the moment his little nose first twitched and his ears first reached up to the sky, Percy loved the wind. While his siblings played tag and hide-and-seek, Percy raced with the wind.

He could hear her. He heard her whisper in the breeze. He heard her roar in the storm.

"Listen. Can't you hear her?" he would ask his brothers, who were too busy trying to tag the next one out.

"Percy, you are just weird. No one talks to the wind."

Their taunting didn't faze him; with each day, his love for the wind grew and grew. He loved her in the summer fields of hollyhocks and roses, blooming in the cottage gardens. He loved her blowing across the springtime heather on the moors. He loved her making the leaves dance in the chilly nights of autumn. And he loved her when the snow was as white as the chalk horse near his burrow.

* * *

Percy grew into a fine young hare, with legs stronger than those of his siblings. No one could outrun him...only the wind could, but she always waited for him to catch up.

"Where do you go?" he would ask.

And the wind would whisper, "Where love goes."

Years passed, and Percy's fur became tinged with white, his whiskers losing their silkiness. His love for the wind only deepened, but now his legs could not run very fast or very far. Most days were spent sleeping in the safety of his burrow.

The wind missed him. She missed their races, but mostly, she missed her friend. Truth be told, the wind loved the old hare. Making the leaves fly wasn't fun any longer. Watching the heather dance across the moor did not delight her without the sound of Percy's laughter.

One morning, she gently caressed the leaves above his burrow, but Percy didn't answer. The wind waited, but the little hare did not stir from his home. Sadly, the wind howled that day, bringing clouds of rain and thunder.

Percy's siblings found him later that afternoon and picked a beautiful spot by the chalk horse to lay him to rest. With tearful eyes, they gathered around his burial mound, their own young families by their sides.

"Where did Percy go?" one of the tiny kits asked, newly born to this world and full of wonder. She raised her whiskers to the slight breeze above her head and twitched her velvety ears toward the sky.

"Hush, Willow. Can't you sit still for just one moment!" her mother chastised. But Willow never sat still. She was always running, from the time her teeny paws hit the ground. Some elders said she reminded them of Percy. Her mother said she was special; her siblings called her weird.

Suddenly, all the hares' noses twitched. Were they imagining it? They felt the ground shake a bit, as if long legs were running across the hill.

"I would swear that was Percy racing by," his brother Oliver gasped.

Just then, Willow heard a quiet voice on the wind. "I went where love goes." Soon, another voice answered, "Yes, I told you I would always wait until you caught up."

Willow looked around. It seemed no one else heard. But she did. She raced off, her tiny paws barely touching the rain-soaked ground, her nose twitching, and her silken whiskers trying to catch the wind.

❧ His Light ❧

Freddie was a lightning bug. But Freddie had no light. Mother told him he was special and it didn't matter, but it did. Freddie knew it. He knew it by the way all the other boy fireflies snubbed him; he sensed it in the way all the girls rolled their bug eyes and quickly flew in the opposite direction.

Freddie decided that he would go on a journey to find his light. He bunched up his pillow to make it look like he was sleeping and set off one summer night while his mother and sisters slept.

He made sure to wear his good sneakers, for he knew he would have far to walk. He crept past his mother's bedroom and peeked in, tears dropping from his round lightning bug eyes. His sisters stirred when his little feet made their floor creak. Freddie just said he was getting a drink of water and for them to go back to sleep. He tiptoed down the stairs and out into the night.

The night was very dark. Freddie didn't have a light to help guide him, and he was trying to convince himself that there was nothing to fear. Suddenly, a voice rang down from a branch above.

"Whooooooooo goes there?"

Freddie answered quietly, "Sorry to disturb you. I am Freddie, and I am searching for my light."

"Your light? Well, that is an arduous journey, Freddie."

"Who are you?" Freddie asked.

"Artemus. Artemus Owl. Why don't you just shine your own light on the path?"

Freddie sighed deeply. "Because I have none. There is something wrong with me."

"Perhaps if you find what is very *right* with you, your light will come," Artemus hooted.

"What do you mean?" Freddie asked.

"You shall see, my friend. You shall see." And with that, and a very loud HOOT, the owl spread his wings and flew off into the night sky.

Freddie was very tired, and his feet ached, even with his good sneakers on. He was hungry, too. Mom would be making a delicious breakfast about now. His tummy growled so loudly that a tiny voice in the grass spoke.

"Who did that?" asked the voice.

Freddie looked down, for the voice was even tinier than his. There, he saw a tiny ant carrying a crumb of bread toward his home.

"It is me, Freddie. I am a lightning bug on a journey to find my light."

"Well now," the ant replied. "Seems a journey like that requires a well-fed tummy. Would you like to share some bread with me?"

Freddie smiled and felt a sudden warmth in his tummy. It was a strange feeling, but one that quickly passed. Together, the two new friends sat down on a patch of moss and shared breakfast.

"Do you know where to find my light?" Freddie asked the ant.

"I know all things in life come from very hard work," said the ant. "You will find your light."

Freddie thanked his friend and said he had to continue on to find the light waiting for him. Off he went; he walked and walked and walked until his tiny feet could not manage another step. He laid his head down in the tall grass and felt a big thump.

"Hey, don't you know it's rude to lie down on top of another!" yelled the voice. Startled, Freddie sprang up to see a long, skinny earthworm. "You nearly squashed me!!!" screamed the worm.

"I am sorry. I didn't mean to. It's...it's just that I am so tired," said Freddie with a big yawn.

"What are you doing in this part of the woods?" the worm asked. "Not many of your kind shine this way."

"I don't shine anyway. I have no light. I am off on a journey to find mine."

"That is some tall adventure," said the worm. "Come rest in my underground burrow for a bit. It isn't much, but it's warm and dry."

So Freddie and the worm bedded down for the night and in the morning shared breakfast before the little bug ventured off again.

"Goodbye, worm. I don't even know your name. What is it?"

"Most just call me worm. That's what I am," he answered.

"Mr. Worm, do you know where my light is?"

"Can't say that I do. I spend all my days in the earth and only come up when the rain comes. Maybe water will bring you light."

"Thank you for sharing your home with me," Freddie called out as he waved his hand goodbye. As he waved, Freddie felt that same sudden warmth surrounding his heart and tummy. And just as soon, it was gone.

Freddie went off in search of water. He walked all day and into the early night. Beside a swamp, Freddie came to a patch of plants, glowing in the darkness. Freddie cried with happiness. "My light! I have found you!!" With that, Freddie tried to wind one of the stalks around his belly.

"Hey, what do you think you're doing?" shrieked the plant.

"I have come to get my light," the little bug cried.

"Not here you don't! I am the Will of the Wisp. I light up this swamp. Who are you?"

"My name's Freddie. I am a lightning bug, but I have no light. No one wants me at my home...well, no one except Mama. I just cannot go back without my light. I have walked for such a long way. I am sorry if I hurt you."

"Artemus warned me I might find you here," Will answered. "Tell you what I will do. Here, wind my wispy arms and legs around your tummy. And no walking. You and I are going to FLY home!"

Freddie wrapped the stalks around his tummy and saw a beautiful glow. "I am just like every other lightning bug now! Thanks, Will!"

Together, the unlikely pair set off in the sky toward home. They flew much of the night, into the next day, and arrived just as the sun was setting. They saw a swarm of flashing lights in the meadow, but none was quite as bright as Freddie's.

Freddie thought of all the friends he had met. He thought of Artemus' strange words. He thought of the kind ant who shared his bread, the bread he had worked so hard to carry home. He thought of the thoughtful worm who shared his tiny home. He especially thought of Will, who gave him his light.

"Will, Will, look!!! Everyone is looking at us and your beautiful light."

But Will wasn't shining anymore. His wispy arms and legs had lost their suppleness, and his eyes were closed.

"Oh no, Will. I should have never let you leave your home."

Freddie's eyes filled with tears. His tears flowed down his chest and all the way down to his tummy. The little bug blazed with the brightest firefly light he had ever seen. He had found what was very right. He had found kindness and thoughtfulness and caring. He had found what was very right in his world, and he had learned what magic the right things in life could give.

Before he headed home to Mama, Freddie searched for a beautiful patch of grass where buttercups bloomed. He laid his tiny friend to rest among the flowers.

Long after the tiny plant stalk had withered back into the earth, a bright light beamed among the buttercups...a light of friendship and gratitude.

Years ago, at my Pennsylvania farmhouse, nights became magickal with the twinkling of hundreds and hundreds of fireflies (or lightning bugs, as some call them). Now, with each passing summer season, the lights grow fewer and fewer. I pray there will never come a summer evening without the glow of these enchanting beings. Whether you are two or ninety-two, their glow is mesmerizing in the darkness.

❦ High Tea ❧

I would love to have tea with a bee

A tea sweetened with honey, you see

We would sit in the shade

And share crumpets he made

And share stories and travels with glee.

I would love to have tea with a bee

In a foresty glade by the sea

Buzzing tales as he poured

Rosehip tea by the shore

What a wonderful day it would be.

I would love to have tea with a bee

In my fanciest skirt at my knee

Not a worry we'd share

Just two friends with no care

How delightful for both him and me.

But, alas, my dream isn't to be

In this world, bees aren't welcomed to tea

Their stingers we fear

Thinking danger is near

How sad how we treat ones so dear.

So, the next time you sweeten your tea

And share crumpets or cupcakes or scones

In a foresty glade

Or backyard in the shade

Think of one little friend

Who toiled in the sun

And gave sweetness to all

You have made.

Yes, I'd love to have tea with a bee

I would thank him and tell him

Well done

For his work here on earth

From the time of his birth

To his last days of toil in the sun.

Written in homage to the bee, so tiny a being, but with so much impact on our earth.

✌ The Call of Love ✍

Jenny was a young hare. She grew up on a lovely, wooded land with her mother, Amelia. Jenny never knew her father. Her mother only said, "He was a seaman; the sea called to him."

Jenny loved her mom. Sometimes, to her dismay, she found her quietly sobbing. Jenny never asked why. She knew. And she hated him. She hated her father, a hare she had never met, had never even known his name.

Years passed, and Jenny grew into a lovely, young maiden.

"I am very ill," her mother whispered one day as the gentle breeze of spring filled the air around them. "I want to take one last trip upon the sea."

"But where, Mother?" Jenny asked.

"I wish to find your father. He never got the chance to know what a beautiful young hare he has in a daughter."

At first, Jenny replied, "I don't want to see him. He left us. All he cared about was the sea. I hate him!!!" But, she saw the sorrow in her mother's brown eyes, eyes that looked so much like her own. "I will take you wherever you wish, Mother."

• • •
18

So, mother and daughter set off in a tiny boat across the sea. Jenny's mom was very weak, too weak for adventures. At night, she coughed and breathed with rasps that worried the young hare.

Days went by, and suddenly, Jenny spotted land. "Mother, Mother, wake up! We are here."

But Jenny's mother did not awaken. Jenny rowed the tiny boat to the island's edge and placed her mother upon a hill of moss beneath the trees. She covered her body with branches and leaves and as many blossoms as she could find in the woodland. Then, afraid and worried what she would do, she fell asleep, exhausted, in a hollow of an ancient tree. She slept for hours, through the day, into the night, and into the next morning. All alone, she could not hold back her tears and wept.

Now, on this island lived a wiry, old hare by the name of Casper. Wizened with age like the ancient tree, his whiskers had grown long and straggly. He wore a seaman's cap and kept a compass on a long chain in his vest pocket.

"Now what have we here?" he shouted.

Jenny looked up, and with fear in her large, brown eyes, she looked into the old hare's wrinkled face. Over a meager breakfast of dug up root vegetables and pinecone seeds, she told him her sad tale.

"Why, you're in luck young lady. I am a seaman. I think I have one last good voyage in me. I will take you home to your grandparents and family."

Jenny didn't fully trust this old hare, but something in the way he looked into her eyes was kind, like he wasn't a stranger. So, he packed his sailor's duffel bag with some food, some water, and a warm blanket for Jenny, and off they went to push his old boat out of storage from under a pile of fallen trees.

"No holes...that's good," Casper exclaimed. "She's still seaworthy. Aye, the sea is calling. Can't you hear her?"

Casper and Jenny set off on their voyage. Each morning, he showed her directions with the rise of the sun. Each evening, he taught her about the constellations and the North Star.

Jenny wished he were her father. She hated *her* father. She must have told Casper that about a hundred times or so.

"Why do you hate him, child?" asked Casper.

"Because he left us."

"The call of the sea is a powerful thing," Casper answered, with wistfulness in his eyes.

Days passed, and Jenny spotted the familiar shoreline of home. Casper gazed out with a bit of déjà vu, feeling like he had seen this place before, a long time ago, when his whiskers were sharp and shiny. He anchored the tiny boat to shore and lifted Jenny out on to the beach.

"This way, Casper. I want you to meet my family."

Casper had a faraway look in his eye. "Jenny, what was your mother's name?"

"Amelia," she answered. "Everyone says I look just like her; I have her eyes. Stay here, Casper. I love you. I wish you were my father."

Casper's eyes glistened in the sunlight as he turned his back from the shoreline. "Aye, my child, the call of the sea is a powerful thing. I have one last voyage in me. Goodbye, sweet child."

With that, Casper stepped aboard his ancient boat and rowed away from the shoreline, never looking back at the little hare. Not because he didn't want to see her, but because he didn't want her to see the tears flowing like waves down his face.

Casper rowed and rowed, not looking at his compass, not searching for the North Star, not gazing at the constellations. His little boat became battered by the currents; his duffel bag became empty of supplies. Exhausted, he closed his eyes and drifted off to sleep. His dreams took him to a beautiful land where a lovely young hare called him father.

A cool breeze drifted across his shoulders and awakened him in the night. A beautiful hare with large, brown eyes sat in the front of the tiny boat.

"Hello, Casper. I have come to take you home."

Casper felt no sadness. For he had learned there is one thing more powerful than the call of the sea...the call of love.

❦ Socks and Fur ❧

Mattie was a tiny mouse. It was her first winter, and she loved snuggling next to Mama and Papa in her cozy nest in a corner of Farmer Will's barn. There were always scraps of rags that Farmer Will left lying around, which Mama chewed tiny pieces from and wove together for warm blankets. Old Farmer Will's soft flannel shirt rags made the coziest blankets.

One especially cold winter morn, Mama told Mattie to stay inside the nest.

"Why?" asked the inquisitive little mouse.

"Because a big snowstorm is coming. I can feel it in my whiskers," Mama answered, her nose twitching in the air.

"What is snow?" Mattie asked. It must be dangerous, she thought. Maybe it's like the big hawk that circles in the sky in the morning. Or maybe it's like the shining eyes of the owl that swoops in the night sky.

"Remember, Mattie, stay inside while Papa and I find some food."

Mattie nodded sleepily and drifted back to slumber. When she opened her eyes, the barn seemed much brighter. All she saw was white through the slats of the barn walls. A strong wind blew something strange into the corners of the floor. Mattie slowly crept to the strange substance and tipped the end of her whisker to it.

"Ouch!" It was sooooooo cold, Mattie's whiskers shivered.

Then, she touched her paw to it; it felt soft as velvet. She licked the tip of her paw and felt the cool taste of it on her tongue. So enthralled, she slipped through the barn slat and ventured outside, forgetting what Mama had told her.

Soon, Mattie was in over her little mouse head as her feet grew tired. "Help, help," she squeaked. But her tiny voice was lost in the wind. Tiny mouse tears turned into icicles as they landed on the snow.

"Well, what have we here?" boomed a loud voice way over her head. It was Farmer Will. Mama told her never to let Farmer Will see her.

"Oh no, why didn't I listen to Mama," she cried.

Farmer Will was a big man; others said he had quite an imposing look about him. But Farmer Will was kind. He knew mice lived in the barn. He knew they chewed his shirts. Each winter, he made sure to leave an old one lying on his tractor in the barn for them to find. Once, he even found a nest inside that tractor, filled with tiny babies. One by one, he lifted the babies out of the nest and placed them in a safe spot before he started the motor. Other farmers used poisons and traps, but Farmer Will thought all little beings deserved a chance to live. And so, he gently scooped little Mattie in his hand and placed his handkerchief around her to keep her warm.

"Come now, little one, let's get you inside to keep warm." He placed Mattie in a cardboard box and carried her back to his farmhouse. Then, he placed a tiny dish of carrots and lettuce and sunflower seeds inside the box and closed the top flap.

Mattie didn't like this dark place. She missed her nest, and she missed Mama and Papa.

When Mama returned to the nest, she found it empty. She was beside herself with worry. Papa returned and was greeted by her frantic sobs. They called and called and searched through all the hay piles, all the rags, and all the corners of the barn. But Mattie wasn't there. They searched until the sun set, until their tired eyes could no longer see. Finally, they went to sleep, fearing their little child had come to great harm.

Mattie, meanwhile, was determined to escape her box. She tried chewing her way out and almost succeeded, but Farmer Will caught her.

"Why, you little rascal," he smiled. "Guess it's a cage for you." And Mattie soon found herself lifted inside a wire cage. "You just wait until the snow clears a bit, little one. Then, I will set you free."

Mattie heard that word again, snow. She hated snow as much as she hated hawk and owl.

Now Farmer Will had a cat, a big orange cat. That cat was as interested in Mattie's cage as Mattie had been with snow. Mattie had seen this cat wandering about the barn. Mama told her never to trust cats, but this big orange one was different. He wasn't a mouser; in fact, he left the little mice alone. That's how he came to live with Farmer Will. The neighbor farmer said the cat flunked the mouser test and was good for nothing. Farmer Will, kind heart that he was, said, "Sure, bring him here."

Mattie was quite a bold little girl. She puffed out her mouse chest and called to the orange beast across the kitchen. "Pssst," she squeaked. "Hey, cat," she called again.

Hearing Mattie, the cat replied, "My name is Toby. Why are you here? Do you know your mama hasn't stopped crying for days? And your papa has been taking a lot of risks in the snow trying to find you. Just yesterday, I had to chase off that big hawk circling above the snow."

"Please tell Mama and Papa I am okay," Mattie squeaked.

When Farmer Will opened the kitchen door to let Toby out, the big, orange cat headed to the barn and told Mattie's parents the snowy tale. That night, he came inside to give Mattie the news.

"Well, they were relieved, but they sure were angry you disobeyed them."

"Toby, please help me get out of here. Farmer Will is going to let me go when the snow clears, but I have never been outside on my own. I am afraid. Please help me."

Farmer Will didn't know Toby knew how to unlatch the kitchen door. In his mind, Toby figured unlatching the cage would be a piece of cake, too. So, that night, the cat opened the cage door and let Mattie out.

"Hop on my back and hold on to my fur."

Mattie jumped on, and Toby opened the kitchen door. A blast of cold air swirled about them, and Mattie held on for dear life as Toby's paws set foot in the snow.

There was a full moon, good for seeing across to the barn, but bad for Toby and Mattie. Owl had better vision than ever under the moonlit sky. They made it halfway across the field when Toby let out a frightening snarl.

"Hold on tight!!!" he screamed.

Toby raced across the field, and Mattie clutched his fur as tightly as her little paws could manage. But it was no use. The owl's talons dug into Toby's neck, lifting him in the air. Mattie fell off in the snow. Toby was too heavy for the owl to manage, and the predator dropped him several feet away from where Mattie fell.

Toby was hurt very badly. Droplets of blood fell from his neck onto the snow. "Go home, Mattie," he whispered. "Go home."

"No, I am not leaving you here to die."

Mattie summoned up all her little mouse courage and ran to the house. She squeezed through the kitchen door, she sniffed her way to Farmer Will's bedroom, and she tugged at his soft pajamas. She tugged and tugged and squeaked so loudly that Farmer Will jumped from his pillow.

"Why, you little rascal. Escaping again, I see!"

But Mattie grabbed his sock and ran. She ran to the kitchen door. She ran through the field.

Now, Farmer Will's wife knitted those socks. She knitted them shortly before she left the farm to join those who came before her. Farmer Will loved those socks. He wasn't giving them up without a fight! Farmer Will ran after Mattie, one sock and slipper on and one sockless foot through the field.

Mattie ran to Toby and licked his face. Farmer Will knelt down beside the orange cat and sighed. "Poor old boy, let's get you inside." He gently scooped the cat up in his arms and carried him to the warm kitchen. He washed his wound and wrapped it in a soft bandage.

"I don't know what happened here. I guess I never will. But I think a little mouse just saved your life, old Buddy."

● ● ●

Mattie smiled a little mouse smile, crept softly to the kitchen door, and squeezed through the bottom crack. She knew about snow now, she knew about hawks and owls, and she knew about the kindness of friends. She went to her parents' nest and hugged them tightly. They did not see their baby looking up into their eyes; they saw a brave, grown mouse.

A baby no longer, Mattie was free to roam the barn and fields and hitch a ride on the back of a furry, orange friend. One day, Farmer Will, upon leaving the barn, left out a pair of soft flannel pajamas and a very special pair of knitted socks, one with a hole in the toe where a tiny mouse had carried it. They were perfect for a little mouse nest, perfect for the babies Mattie soon would have.

Woven into that nest, there might also be some tufts of orange fur, snatched during hitchhiked rides. A nest filled with the coziness of love and kindness. Mattie would warn her babies of the hawks, the owls, the snow. But she knew they would have to face their own dangers, and hope for the kindness of friends...some with fur, some without.

I have been lucky to be the mom to several mice—Mr. Bumbles, Miss Charlotte Bumbles, Blaze (because he had a white stripe, or blaze, down his forehead like Lassie), and

Harry Potter. They each had their own unique personality, their own likes, and each made a big mouse hole in my heart when their short mouse lives were done.

❦ A Nuisance ❧

Gabby was a tiny gosling. She and her siblings lived on a little pond in the middle of a park with their mom and dad. A lot of people walked by the pond; some tossed bits of bread or popcorn in the water, but some of the people hated her family. They just shouted at the mess these geese make in the park. They put up signs to not feed them. They petitioned the town to get rid of them all.

Gabby grew stronger each day and could swim back and forth across the pond many times without tiring. She became an excellent swimmer and could dive her head under the water, looking for food.

One day, a group of boys came to the park. The feathers on Gabby's back perked up, sensing danger. These boys weren't kind. She saw them picking up rocks. And she saw them throwing them in the water...at her and her family!

Her parents huddled them together, but they were no match. Four of Gabby's siblings were fatally struck. Her mother and father were struck, as well, trying to save them. Only Gabby and her sister Gretchen were left. The boys heard people coming and ran off laughing. Gabby and Gretchen held each other's wings and sobbed.

"Why?" asked Gretchen.

Gabby shook her head. "Humans can be kind, and humans can be cruel," she answered.

From that day on, Gabby and Gretchen swam at the far side of the pond where large waterweeds grew. They never came out for crumbs and only walked on the shore in the moonlight when no humans were around. Gretchen soon met a handsome male and chose him for a mate. Gabby was left alone.

Winter was coming, and most of the geese were leaving the pond. Gabby chose to stay behind, in the place where her family had been so happy. Winter was very harsh, and Gabby grew very thin. Not many people came to the park; those that did hurried on the path and had no care for a frail, little goose.

One day, Gabby caught her wing in the stalk of weeds and broke it. She could not fly; she could only hobble from the water to the shore. She could not run or swim fast from rocks anymore.

Some time later, a woman with grey hair came to the water's edge and called to Gabby. She had peas and corn and bits of crackers in her purse. "I know I am not supposed to feed you," she whispered. "But I cannot stand to see you hungry."

"My house is just up from the hill. I watch you every day. And I see you in the moonlight all alone. I am alone, too," she sighed. "Maybe we can be alone together."

Gabby didn't try to swim away. She didn't have the strength anymore. So, she hobbled to the woman's feet and gently took the food.

"There," the woman said. "I will come tomorrow. Wait for me."

Tomorrow, she came. And the next day, and the next, and the next, and many days after that. She came all of January, all of February, all of March, and into the coming spring. Gabby loved the woman. She waited each morning and gave a big honk when she saw her coming. Her wing never properly healed, but she was walking easier.

One day, a van pulled up by the park entrance and men in uniforms came to the shore. "That's her," one of them said, pointing to Gabby. "That's the sick goose we have gotten complaints about; he must be full of disease." They carried a long pole with a hook at the end and reached for Gabby.

Suddenly, the old woman came hurrying as fast as she could to the edge of the lake. "What are you doing!!!!"

"Town orders, ma'am. Please back away, we have to catch this one."

The old woman's pleas gave Gabby enough time to swim away. She hid in the tall weeds.

"It must have flown away," one of the men surmised. "Let's go to the other side of the park and try to get him!"

Relieved, the old woman called to her friend. "Come, come with me. Hurry!"

Gabby came out from the weeds. The old woman scooped her up in her arms and hid her beneath her long, woolen coat. She carried her into her home and into her warm kitchen.

"We won't tell anyone you're here," she whispered. "At night, you can go for a swim in the moonlight. No one visits me. My children have forgotten me. We will always be alone together," she said as she smiled tenderly down at the goose.

Spring turned into summer, and the old woman tended a garden with delicious vegetables. Behind the tall, wooden fence, no one saw Gabby. When geese flew overhead, the old woman told her to be quiet, and Gabby never let out a honk. The old woman ordered a kiddie pool on the Internet and didn't bat an eye as the postman gave her a funny glance.

Gabby and her friend lived through the summer and into the autumn happily. Soon, though, the old woman could no longer walk very well. She couldn't take Gabby out to the pond anymore for moonlight swims. She hobbled very much like the young goose once did.

● ● ●

One day, the woman opened her kitchen door and said to Gabby, "Be free." Gabby refused to move. The woman kept insisting and insisting, but Gabby stayed put and honked very loudly for the first time in months.

The woman grew weaker and weaker with each day. She couldn't shop anymore. Finally, when mail started piling up outside her door, the mailman called the town police. When they entered, they saw an unusual sight. The old woman had died in her bed, surrounded by bits of crackers and pieces of dried fruits and vegetables. The remains of a tiny goose lay on the floor by her bedside.

"Disgusting creatures," one of the policemen sighed. "Probably carried a lot of disease."

"Yeah," his partner added. "We should rid this town of all of them."

The old woman's children were called. "What? She had a goose in the house! She must have been senile," they replied. "I can just imagine the mess we will have to clean up before we sell the place!"

They saw a pest; they saw disease; they saw a nuisance. What they didn't see was two beings alone together, until the very end of their days.

I would always go to my town park and feed the geese. Some familiar ones I learned to recognize and vice versa. One special goose hobbled to one side with a broken wing. I looked for him each day and made sure he got his share of food. One day, large signs went up that feeding was NOT allowed. Methods to eradicate the geese were implemented in town. There was a beautiful family of geese in the water. One day, they were gone; I heard people talking that some boys had thrown rocks and killed them. I have never forgotten that horrible day.

∾ Paw Prints in the Snow ∾

Once upon a time, a lonely little girl longed for a friend. She was the only child of a village miller and his wife. Hard work filled her parents' days, and sleep descended upon their eyes with the coming of each night.

Hester was born with one leg shorter than the other; she walked with a very bad limp. She could not make the long walk to the village school, and her papa was too busy in the mornings grinding wheat at his mill to drive her in his horse-drawn cart. They were poor people and gave their daughter as much as they could provide with their meager funds. But, they could not give her the one thing for which her heart longed most.

Hester's mom was busy tending the farm and the kitchen, but she would spend a little time each day with studies, teaching the little girl to read. Books were cherished possessions; Hester read and reread each of the dog-eared pages of books her mom had given her. Friends in the pages of the stories comforted her, but Hester longed for a real friend.

Village children could be cruel. On Sundays, Hester would go to church service with her parents. She would hear the quiet snickers of the village children, dressed in their fine Sunday best, teasing over her muslin smock and laughing at the way her feet moved. Hester would quietly sob in her room when they made the trip home again.

Winters were especially lonely. Her parents' work eased a bit, but worries filled their minds, not fun and games to lighten a daughter's sad heart. Walking in the snow was especially hard, and the ill-fitting, hand-me-down boots Hester wore offered little help. But she was a good daughter, and each day, she would trudge to the well and gather water for her mother to make tea at the hearth fire.

One morning, Hester looked down and saw a strange set of prints. She knew all the animals in the snow. She could identify the tiny bird tracks; she could tell the hoof prints of the deer and fawns; and she could recognize the swooping wing marks the owls and hawks made in the snow as they searched for food. This set of tracks was different. Part of it looked like it belonged to a tiny animal. Another part looked like a paw print but stretched long and deep, as if something was dragged in the snow. She followed the tracks with her eyes to the nearby trees, but her mother called from the farmhouse door for her to come inside with the water bucket.

All day, Hester thought about those tracks. She wasn't allowed to go beyond the nearby trees at the edge of the miller's property, and Hester never disobeyed before. But this time...something called to her. A strange feeling came over her, a feeling Hester didn't understand, a feeling deep within her heart. She knew she had to follow the prints; she had to see who made them.

The next morning, Hester went out to the well again. Snow had fallen in the night, covering up the strange prints. Hester searched and searched and found a new set, this time wandering into the barn! Hester trudged through the fresh snow and looked inside.

"Hello? Where are you?" she called.

Hester adjusted her vision to peer inside the dark barn. She saw her mother's old milking cow and her father's carthorse. Nothing else seemed unusual.

Then, she heard a strange whimpering coming from a mound of hay. A pair of sad, brown eyes looked up at the little girl. It was hard to tell that a little dog lay beneath the matted fur and snow clumps that hung on his legs and tummy.

"Oh, you poor little one!" Hester cried. She held out her hands, and the little dog slowly crept toward them. Hester saw one of his legs was bent at a strange angle as he dragged it behind him. "You walk just like me," she said lovingly.

The little dog's shivers of fear eased, and he extended a small, pink tongue to lick Hester's hand. She scooped him up in her arms and brought him back to the kitchen.

"What is that dirty thing doing in my kitchen?" her mother shrieked when she saw the matted bundle sleeping by the hearth.

"Please, Mama, he is cold and hungry. Can we feed him?"

Papa came inside for his tea and yelled to get that dirty mongrel OUT!

The little dog slowly stood up, dragging his bent leg across the floor and tucking his tail between his legs, and crept toward the door. Mama saw the leg; Papa stared at the dragging foot. "Hester, we will need extra buckets of water to heat at the fire," said Papa. Mama reached for some towels. "Yes, he will need a bath."

That next Sunday, Mama, Papa, Hester, and the little dog climbed into the horse-drawn cart and went to church. The little dog stayed in the cart, waiting for his friend to return. As always, the village children snickered, giggled, and lifted their noses in snobbery. But Hester didn't care. She had all that she ever wanted, a friend.

The dog waited many winters to follow, always at the feet of the little girl whose heart belonged to him. To him, she

• • •

couldn't be more beautiful. To her, he was the most perfect little dog in the world.

❦ The Rose ❧

O nce upon a time, the loveliest blossom grew in the forest. Her crown was red, with lovely petals soft as velvet and fragrance as sweet as a summer's day. Each time one of the villagers passed, the urge to pick her blossoms was overwhelming. The tired plant grew weary of having all her flowers torn from her stems.

One day, a tiny fairy landed on one of her blossoms. "Please, Fairy, I have a favor to ask," the plant whispered. "Please take my beauty. Take my perfume and replace it with a smell that turns noses away from my stem," the weary plant asked.

The fairy was so taken by the beauty of this plant that she could not bear to honor this request. "I cannot do this. You are so lovely; you are a gift to the forest. Your fragrance brings the bees and butterflies—my friends. And your lovely red color brings the hummingbirds—my sisters—to your stems."

The blossom shook her petals in understanding. The fairy went home and spoke to her elders about the weary blossom's plea.

In the morning, the fairy returned and sprinkled fairy dust on top of the blossoms. Instantly, prickly thorns sprouted along her stems, and briars toughened her winding branches.

"It will be harder for others to pick your blooms now," she whispered. "But my friends and sisters will still find you in the forest."

"Thank you," nodded the rose, as tears of dew fell from her petals. And to this day, every rose bears this fairy's gift.

❧ The Stash of Coins ❧

One day, a farmer was bringing his crops to market when he spotted a ragged, burlap bag on the side of the road. "Should I stop?" he wondered aloud to himself. After a second's pondering, he told his old horse, "Whoa," and stepped down to investigate the contents of this bag.

It was tied with twine and knotted so tightly he had trouble opening it. He tried to drag it to his cart. It weighed a ton and jingled. By now, his imagination was swirling with riches; this sounded like coins! Could this be? Could his fortunes have changed so suddenly?

As he opened the bag, the coins glimmered in the sun like jewels. The farmer hurried to his cart and lifted the bag, covering it with sacks of potatoes. No market for him today! He hurried home to bury his stash in his field.

Times were very hard that harvest. His potatoes would have barely provided enough money to feed him through the winter. Now, he had no worries.

The townspeople, though, were starving. Their potatoes were rotten, as well, and they had no bag of coins to hide away. They mustn't know, he resolved. The farmer hoarded his wealth. He took only a few coins at a time, and he rode all the way out to three distant villages so others would not know of his ability to splurge and live "high on the hog."

Babies in his village were sick and dying. Beggars pleaded on the roadside as he passed for just a crumb of bread. The farmer turned his head and kept on driving by with his cart, faster with each plea. On return trips, he covered his food with old, dirty blankets and piled dirt on top so others would not steal. Stragglers would come calling at his door, smelling his hearth fires cooking. But the farmer just bought several strong locks for his door.

Then, the farmer became worried about his gold in the field. He worried someone would watch and steal it away in the night. Under a moonless sky, he dragged the bag into his home and pried up several floorboards to hide his secret.

Each time he went to market, he bought another lock, and another, and another. Soon, his door was covered in them. He carried a large ring of keys on his belt that jingled as he rode past travelers lying on the roadside.

One frigid night, while the farmer was cooking his dinner, a knock came upon the door. "Please, may I come in, sir, just to warm these tired, old bones?"

"Go away!!!" shouted the farmer.

"Please, sir. I smell food cooking. I am just a poor traveler who suffered great misfortune last harvest season when bandits stole all the money collected for my village. I was delivering it to the landlord, and I was blamed for stealing it, though I did no such thing. I cursed the bandits who took it and wished them a terrible, suffering death. All I have to my name are a few pennies. Listen," said the traveler as he jingled them in his pocket. "All that I have is yours. You may have every penny."

"Go away!" the farmer repeated. "I don't need your measly pennies!"

After a few minutes and no reply, the farmer laughed to himself, "Stupid old man. Your misfortune is my fortune!" And with those words, he began to pry up the floorboards to count his gold again.

He laid the boards against the hearth and began counting. He was so enthralled with the glittering coins that he did not notice the spark land on one of them. Before he realized it, the room was ablaze in fire!

The farmer started toward the door. But there were so many locks! He opened one, then another. The flames shot closer and closer. His shaking hands fumbled for the next and the next and the next.

But it was too late.

Villagers came upon the ruins of his farmhouse and a melted heap that glistened in the sun. Alongside it sat a ring of metal keys, melted together in the flames. They jingled no more.

"Why, I think this is gold!!!" shouted one of them. The others gathered 'round, not believing what sat before them. One villager took out an old, ragged burlap bag and placed the heap inside it. The bag did not jingle this time, for it was just one solid mass of gold. They sent one young man to take the riches to the landlord and pay off all their debts.

Little did they know, a cold and very tired traveler sat upon the hill, watching. He jingled the pennies in his pocket and grinned.

✤ Food for Her Soul ✤

In the back of Bryant's small general store lived a tiny mouse named Flora. She slept in an old flour sack with her mother, father, and three sisters. Flora was quite a social mouse. She had many friends—some, like Christopher Ant, who lived in the store, and some, like Mortimer Monarch, who lived in the park outside and sometimes flew in for a snack of sugar.

Flora longed to see the outside world. Her mother and father told her the outside world was a dangerous place; it was much safer to stay in the quiet darkness of the back storeroom.

"Why should you leave? We have everything we need here," said her mama. "We have food, warmth, and a safe place, as long as we avoid the traps in the corners."

But Flora spoke to Christopher of the trails he had taken through ant tunnels that led to adventures all across the town. And she spoke to Mortimer about his flights all the way to Mexico, wherever that place was. Mortimer said it was beautiful, a place where instead of leaves, the trees grew butterflies! Mortimer filled Flora's head with stories of geese in flight and hummingbirds that stretched their tiny wings across the continent. Flora could only stretch her tiny mouse feet across the dust-filled floor.

Weeks passed, and Flora was old enough to stretch her mouse feet further. Despite Mama's worrying, she packed a little bag of food and set off to the park where Mortimer lived. What wonders she beheld! Giant trees, big enough for every mouse in the world to call home, surrounded her. Puddles of water, so much bigger than the spots of rain that leaked from Mr. Bryant's roof, sparkled in the sunlight. Flora had only seen sunlight streaming through the dust from a tiny window in the storeroom. Now, she felt her head grow warm as it fell upon her fur.

Mortimer introduced her to all his buddies. Sammy Caterpillar was busy finding tender leaves; Charlie Cricket was busy chirping for a mate. Sandra was a beautiful, white snow goose. She told Flora she had traveled the skies for thousands of miles.

"Oh, how lucky you are," exclaimed Flora, "to have journeyed to so many distant places. I wish I could go with you."

"My days of flight have ended," sighed Sandra, showing Flora the broken feathers of an injured wing. "I wish I had a nice safe home to rest in."

Mortimer introduced Flora to Freddie Squirrel. "Oh yes," Freddie squeaked. "I have been to many parks and lived inside many trees. This park has a kind man who sits on that bench every morning and feeds me peanuts. It's nice to have a home where food awaits my hungry tummy each morning. You are so lucky to live in a store!"

Flora went home, still not happy with her tiny nest in the back storeroom. Yes, she had food and she had shelter, but her heart longed for more. Just what that was, Flora did not know. Mama had taught her some letters; she could read the labels on Mr. Bryant's shelves, and she knew which letters spelled P-O-I-S-O-N. But Flora wanted to learn more. She wanted to see the fields as Sandra did, flying overhead. She wanted to see the place where millions of Mortimers lived.

The next morning, Flora set out to the park again. She hid under the bench that Freddie had pointed to, and, sure enough, a white-haired gentleman sat down. (Flora could tell this man was different from Mr. Bryant. For one thing, Mr. Bryant had no hair. Also, Mr. Bryant would not have a bag of food waiting to feed mice, that's for sure. Each time he went into the storeroom, all of the mice had to hide.) The white-haired man carried a backpack. He reached in and got out a bag full of peanuts.

On cue, Freddie peeped his head out of his tree nest and scurried to the man's feet. "Hey, what are you doing here?" he squeaked to Flora. But before she could answer, he stuffed three peanuts in his mouth and ran off.

The man took a book out of his backpack and started to read. Flora could see letters on the cover. She so wanted to learn more letters! Flora tucked her little mouse body inside the man's backpack and hid. Soon, she was swinging from side to side as the man walked home.

It was very dark inside the backpack, and Flora had no idea where she was going. Then, the bag crashed to the ground with a THUD! The man reached in, grabbed his book, and did not zip up the top. Flora listened as his footsteps got farther and farther away. Then, she peeked her head out of the bag and looked around.

It was like Mr. Bryant's storeroom, but books filled the shelves. Books of all sizes, all colors, with letter after letter after letter written on the fronts. Flora had never seen so many letters before! She spotted a bright red book with ABCs written on the cover. She crept into a dark corner of the shelf, after taking a few peanuts out of the backpack for lunch, and waited until the store became very quiet. Then, she set off on her adventure to see the world.

There was a little room in back with a teakettle and some cookies. Flora helped herself to the crumbs of a broken one, then hurried back to find the red book. Flora tried sounding out each letter, but it was so very hard. Then, a "psssst" came from another shelf.

"Who are you?" asked a tiny voice.

"I am Flora," she answered.

"I'm Tillie," the voice replied. "I live here in the bookstore."

"A bookstore?" Flora cried. "You mean instead of food, the white-haired man sells books?"

"Well, books are kind of like food," Tillie answered. "Food for the soul. That's what my papa used to say."

"Do you know how to read all these books?" Flora asked.

"Sure, my papa taught me. You can learn all kinds of stuff if you know how to read."

"Can you learn about the place where butterflies fill the trees like leaves?"

"Oh, you mean Mexico?" Tillie squeaked.

"Yes, Mexico!!!" cried Flora.

"C'mon," said Tillie. "I will show you where my nest is." So, Flora followed Tillie to a high shelf at the back of the store. "No one ever takes down a book from here. During the day, I keep quiet, but at night, I can look at any book I want. I can travel the world."

Flora's eyes grew big as saucers. "Tillie, can I stay here with you? Will you teach me how to read about the world?"

Tillie smiled. "C'mon, I know where Mr. Peters keeps all his bags of peanuts and cookies. It will be nice to have a friend. By the way, how did you hear about Mexico?"

Flora began to tell her new friend all about Mortimer as the two of them scampered along the shelves to the back of the bookshop. Tillie listened intently, her mouth stuffed with butter cookie crumbs.

There were a few ants raiding the cookie shelf. Flora requested that they get word to Christopher and ask him to tell Mama and Papa she was safe. The ants shook their antennae and scurried off, carrying their crumbs.

Flora was safe, and she had food. Food for her tummy...and food for her soul.

❧ Night Song ❧

One June morning

Two little cicadas awoke from their slumber.

When their red eyes met

It was love at first sight.

"I will love you forever," said one to the other.

"We will share sunrises and sunsets

 And sunshine and moonlight."

And they did.

They shared a lifetime of sunrises....

A lifetime of sunsets....

They went for walks in the grass.

He sang her sweet songs of love.

And the weeks were their years....

And when their month in the sun

Had come to its end....

They kissed one another goodbye

And closed their red eyes

 As their last sun set

And went to slumber

As the full moon rose,

On their last night song of love.

If you are ever fortunate to be in an area when the cicadas emerge from their seventeen-year slumber, you will never forget the sound and sight of these beings. I have held them in my hands. They are gentle and bring no harm to humans, who fear their existence for no true reason. Hold one, gaze into his large, red eyes, and meet a fellow traveler in the Universe.

✌ The Little Artist ✍

O nce upon a time, in a woodland of tall oaks and flowering bluebells, lived a tiny robin named Rose. Rose loved to paint; she painted rocks and branches, bark of trees, and any scrap of trash blown into the woodland. Tiny mice collected their fallen whiskers and gave them to Rose to make into brushes on twigs. Silkworms spun fine silk to make beautiful paper that Rose only used for very special pieces of art.

One day, a man passing through the woodland came upon one of Rose's paintings. The tiny piece of beautiful artwork fascinated the man, who only thought of greed and riches. "Why, I imagine the King would pay a fine price for this," he said aloud. No one was around, or so he thought. But the mice were hiding in the dry leaves and overheard. They saw the man pick up Rose's painting and put it in his satchel. Rose was heartbroken that the man had stolen her painting; it was a very special one, painted on silkworm silk.

The thief brought the tiny painting to the King, who absolutely loved it. "My daughter, Princess Leslie, will love this! Did you paint this?"

"Yes," lied the man in reply.

"Splendid, you will become the Palace artist. If you can paint *this* tiny treasure, imagine what you can create on the large Palace walls! Get your things, you will move into the Palace at the end of the week. Your first commission will be due in one month, in time for the Palace fancy gala."

The man knew he was in trouble now. He couldn't draw a stick figure! He decided to hide out in the woodland and see who painted the beautiful creation. He made himself a tent of branches and leaves, tucked himself away from view, and waited. He waited all day and all night.

The next morning, little Rose set up her twig easel in the sunlight, took out her mouse whisker brushes, and started to paint. The man's eyes twinkled with glee.

"I will set a trap by moonlight. Tomorrow, this little artist will be mine."

And so he did. Rose was unaware of the danger waiting. She set up her easel and was just about to paint her first stroke when a net from a branch above fell on her tiny head and covered her body. She was trapped!

"Help, help," she chirped.

But her friends could only watch as the man stuffed her, the easel, and her paints into his satchel. The tiny mice followed behind, watching the man come to a crumbling shack at the edge of the village and disappear within.

"Now, my little artist, you will work for me," said the man. He placed Rose inside a cage and shoved her art supplies inside. "Now, paint me a beautiful picture!"

Rose was shaking. Her tiny feet tried to hold the brush, but she kept dropping it onto the cage floor.

"Either you paint a picture for me or you will never live to paint a picture again!!" he screamed.

Rose painted a tall, black oak, with shriveled branches drooping in the woodland.

"This isn't what you painted before," said the man. "Where are the bright colors? I cannot give the King this for his daughter. He would have me hanging from that miserable tree! Paint another, and make it better this time."

Rose painted, her tears dripping onto the paper and blurring the colors together.

"You have one last chance, little bird. Make it good!!!"

So, Rose painted a beautiful, blue sky with robins flying beneath the clouds.

"That's better," he chortled. "The King will like this one. Hurry, make more. I have to pack my things. You are coming with me to the Palace tomorrow. I will have you paint in the night so no one will know it is you, not me, who creates such beauty."

By now, the mice had chewed their way into a corner of the man's shack and listened in horror. "Once Rose goes inside the Palace, we will never be able to free her. The Palace walls are chew proof. We have to act tonight!" The mice ran back to the woodlands to get help. They would need a lot of help to free their friend.

They summoned the rats who lived by the pond to come and help chew the wooden cage bars with them. They asked the opossum to carry all of Rose's art supplies in her pouch. All creatures of the night joined in the escape plan, waiting until the man was fast asleep.

"Rose, Rose, wake up," whispered one of the mice. "Rose, wake up. We have to get you out of here."

The mice and rats scurried across the floor and climbed onto the table where Rose's cage sat. They began chewing and chewing until a hole big enough to fit Rose emerged. Forming a rodent pyramid, the creatures climbed to the door latch and unhooked it. The door was heavy, but together, they pushed and pushed until the opossum could squeeze through. She packed all of Rose's art supplies inside her pouch.

"Wait," said Rose to the opossum. "Please take these, too." And Rose placed all of her finished paintings inside the pouch with the twig easel and paints.

When the man awoke, the robin, the paint, and the paintings were gone. The King's guards knocked at his door. "Come with us now to the Palace. The King is waiting."

When they got to the Palace, the King had set up a beautiful art room for the man. The finest silk paper, the best colors in every hue imaginable, and a tall easel made of the sturdiest oak.

"Now paint!" the King ordered.

"Oh, Your Majesty, I forgot something very important at my house. Don't bother your guards. I will go fetch it and be back by tonight."

"My gala is soon; I want these paintings finished in time," said the King.

"Yes, Your Majesty," the man answered.

The man raced from the Palace gates and ran into the woodland where he had captured Rose. The mice, the rats, and the opossum watched as he raced from tree to tree, sweat pouring from his brow, with no luck finding her. He could not go home; the Palace guards would be looking for him.

He was trapped. The woodland had become his cage, and no friends would be coming to release him. Without food, without any supplies, the man wandered through the tall oaks until his strength was gone.

When he awoke, the Palace guards were staring down at him. "The King is very angry. Come with us!" they demanded. And they brought the man back to stand before the King.

* * *

"Your Majesty, I cannot paint. I stole that painting from a tiny robin in the woods."

The King looked at the man with pity. The guards doubled over in laughter. "A robin? He thinks a robin is the artist!!"

The man was deemed insane and placed inside a tiny dungeon in the Castle basement. It had bars on the window, like a tiny cage.

The King tossed in some old brushes, paint, and a splintery, old easel. "Now paint," he chuckled in jest.

⸙ Gilda ⸰

Gilda was a little ghost. She lived in an abandoned farmhouse at the end of a long, dirt road. Down the dirt road was the town cemetery. Gilda never left her farmhouse, but sometimes, she peered out the upstairs bedroom window—well, it used to be a window before the glass shattered—and looked out across the field to the cemetery. She always got a weird feeling when she saw that place, weird even for a ghost.

Gilda knew she was a ghost, but she didn't belong in that cemetery. This farmhouse was her home. This was all she knew. When she looked at the walls, she didn't see cracks; she saw lovely, flowered wallpaper, adorned with beautiful, red roses. When she looked at the floor, she didn't see dust and dried leaves blown in from the outside; she saw beautiful patterned rugs, in shades of pinks and creams and blues.

Sometimes, older kids from town would wander into the farmhouse and play tricks upon each other. Gilda didn't like that. She didn't like scaring people. Most times, she just hid in the attic until they were gone.

• • •

But sometimes, they stayed long into the night. Gilda wanted to be alone, and sometimes, she stamped her ghost feet loudly to make them go. And go they did, running from the parlor, down the front steps so fast that they often fell along the broken risers.

One day, one of the kids lit a cigarette in the farmhouse and tossed it on a pile of leaves that had gathered on the floor. Gilda got to it just in time and blew her icy ghost breath upon the flames. The others just watched, scared out of their wits, as the mist blew across the room. After that, no one came and disturbed her again. Until that Tuesday....

Gilda thought it was a Tuesday. She often counted the days from when the town church bells rang on Sunday. Sometimes, she got mixed up when the town had a funeral and rang the bells. Then, Gilda would peer out the window and see the long row of cars drive through the cemetery gates.

Gilda didn't like funeral days. They sent a cold shiver down her ghostly spine. She was home. This was her home. This was her kitchen, where the dented, old teakettle still looked shiny and bright. This was her garden, where roses, not weeds, bloomed before her eyes. This was her forever.

Then, that Tuesday morning, the man and woman came. They walked up the rickety front steps, the man tossing one of the boards across the front yard. They walked inside the parlor, and the woman ran her fingers across the dust-laden mantle, blowing the dust moats through the air.

Gilda didn't like this, not one bit. She glided up the stairs to the attic and started stamping her feet louder than she had ever done before. But the man and woman still kept wandering around.

"There's a ghost here," the woman said with a smile. "I knew this place must have some spirits."

"Well, lucky for them, we bought this place. Now they will have someone to talk to," her husband answered.

The woman just smiled. She walked to the bedroom window and sensed all those times Gilda had looked through the open frame. Her eyes drifted to the cemetery down the road.

"She is there—well, her body is," she told her husband. "I am going to take a walk through that cemetery when we leave."

Gilda hovered over, listening intently. Who was this woman, and why wasn't she afraid? How did she know where Gilda's body was? Gilda never left the farmhouse, but this time, she followed the man and woman as they got into their car.

"Someone is still with us," the woman whispered.

"No one harmful, I hope," the man answered with worry in his voice.

"No, not harmful. Just a lost soul."

"Well, lost souls always find you, or you find them," her husband sighed.

When they got to the cemetery gates, Gilda shuddered. The man and woman got out and started walking around. Gilda hovered nearby.

"This way, I think this is where she was laid to rest." Walking among the tangled ivy and crumbling headstones, the woman came to a small cross. Much of the writing had worn away, but part of a name was still readable. "Gilda....born 18 something. I cannot make it out."

Gilda looked down at the cross. All of a sudden, memories came flooding back. Memories of a little girl, sick with fever in that bedroom. Memories of a mother and father staring down at her bed, with tears in their eyes. Too many memories to bear. "No, no, I want to go home." And Gilda flew across the fields and into the farmhouse again.

Weeks passed, and the man and woman came every day to the farmhouse. They started cleaning and filling in cracks and painting. They repaired the glass windows. The man repaired all of the broken wooden risers on the front porch steps.

Then, one morning, the woman reached for Gilda's teapot and tossed it in the trash.

"Stop!" yelled Gilda. "That is mine. This house is mine."

The woman smiled. "I knew you would eventually come to me," she whispered, with kindness in her voice. She lifted a beautiful new teapot out of a box on the floor. "This is my teapot. This is my farmhouse now. You are welcome to stay, but you know you don't belong here anymore, don't you? I know your name is Gilda, isn't it? I can help you if you let me. I can help you find your parents again."

Gilda ran and hid in the attic. She was afraid. Through the attic window, she gazed out to the cemetery. She didn't want to go there, among the tangled ivy and crumbling stones. She wanted to stay with her roses and with her precious teapot, now in the garbage.

"Gilda, Gilda, let me help. I promise, you don't have to be afraid."

Gilda saw a lovely light come through the attic window. She heard the woman's footsteps climbing the attic stairs.

"I know you are here, Gilda. I have always known you were here. You don't belong here anymore. You belong back with those who love you. Just follow that light," the woman called. "Take just one step, and you will see."

Gilda felt warmth in that light. She felt a love she had not felt for so long. In the distance, she saw a farmhouse. Her farmhouse. The roses bloomed in reds and pinks and yellows. The window glass sparkled in the sunlight. She walked farther into the light, up the front steps, which were no longer broken and crumbling. Her feet touched the softness of a beautiful, pink carpet in a room where blossoms adorned the papered walls and crystal vases lined the dust-free mantel.

Then, a soft voice called from the kitchen. "Come, Gilda, it's time for tea." Her mother held a gleaming teapot in her hands and poured tea into a beautiful porcelain teacup. For the first time in over a century, Gilda was home. "We have been waiting for you, Gilda."

"Hi, honey. Where are you? What happened today?" came the man's voice from the parlor.

"I'm up in the attic. I will be right down," said the woman. She came into the kitchen and kissed him hello as she grabbed two porcelain cups from the cupboard.

"So, how was your day?" he asked. "Save any lost souls?"

"One little one," she answered with a smile as she put the kettle on the stove for tea.

"It's good to be home," he sighed. "It's been a long night shift," he added as he sat down at the kitchen table.

Just then, the town church bells rang out in the distance.

"Another soul has crossed. May this spirit travel in peace," she sighed, as she poured the steaming tea into their cups.

Some nights, as she lay awake in bed, the woman thought she felt a slight breeze ruffling the lace curtains of her room, though she knew the bedroom windows were shut. "Gilda," she would whisper, "you know you are always welcome here. Make yourself a nice cup of tea. There are some freshly baked cookies on the table. Bring some home with you."

Beautiful roses always bloomed at Gilda's tiny cross. A little garden sign read *Come for Tea* at the side of her grave. Others might find this sign odd, but the young woman who often visited didn't think so. She thought it absolutely perfect.

✎ Unique ✎

Once upon a time, a family of foxes lived on the heathered fields in England. Papa Fox would go out for food each day, while Mama Fox would sit in the den with her pups.

Foxes weren't liked; they were looked upon as thieves and mischievous intruders who only caused damage to property and chickens.

Most hated them, but Sarah was different. She loved them. She thought them to be so beautiful. Her hair was red like theirs, so she felt a kinship with their kind. To her, they were family.

One day, Sarah came upon a fox wounded on the side of the road. Exhausted, he had run from the hounds with all his strength; Sarah could still hear them baying on the trail.

"Oh, you poor thing! Come with me." Sarah lifted the half-dead fox in her arms and carried him back to her home. She placed him on a rug in the shed and put out water and food for him. Then she went back inside her cottage.

The poor fox was too exhausted to drink or eat and fell deeply into sleep. He didn't hear the hounds barking wildly at Sarah's gate.

A knock upon Sarah's door caused her to jump. It was a hunter. The sound of hounds and hunters always sent shivers down her spine.

"Have you seen a fox on your property? You know, a wounded animal can be quite dangerous. We best have a look around. I never see my hounds this agitated unless one of those foxes is near."

"I don't think so. This is private property. Please get off my land and take your hunting party with you!" Sarah answered.

In a huff, the man walked through the gate and got back on his horse, muttering something about the anger of redheads. He signaled the other men and hounds to follow.

Sarah was worried to open her shed the next morning, afraid that the fox had not survived the night. But, when she did, she saw the fox had revived and was staring thankfully into her eyes. She knew he wasn't going to harm her; she could see he only wanted to get back out into the field, back to his wife and pups. He must have family waiting, Sarah thought to herself.

"Go on, it's safe now."

The fox darted quick as a flash past the garden gate and into the heather.

Sarah lived alone. Her parents had died when she was a baby, and a loving family had adopted her. Sarah felt loved, but never in the same way. She was always referred to as the "mischievous redhead." Now, living alone suited her; Sarah liked it that way. (The nearest neighbor was three miles down the road.) Nevertheless, being alone can pose its dangers.

One day, out in the garden, Sarah fell and hit her head on a large, sharp-edged stone. She felt dizzy each time she tried to stand and knew she could not make it to her door to call for help.

From out in the heather, Papa Fox was telling a tall tale about the kind human who saved him. His little pups sat wide-eyed with wonder as he wove a tale of horses and hounds and hunters. Suddenly, Papa Fox's keen eyes saw the kind human lying on the ground in her garden. His keen nose sensed human blood. She was hurt.

Papa Fox told his pups to hide in the very tall heather and stay quiet. He told them under no circumstances were they to move.

Then, Papa Fox did something quite magical. Now, few people know that foxes are shape shifters. They can change into beings using the magic of ancient ways. The pups saw a tall man with flowing, red hair (tied back into a long ponytail) emerge before their eyes. Sarah was unconscious and did not see the human stop at her side and touch her forehead with his hand.

Then, Papa Fox went into the cottage, looking for any clothing that might fit. He found an old, denim shirt and cotton trousers that hung in a closet. They would have to do. There was little time. He ran down the road until he came to the first cottage he saw. Knocking on the door, he said the kind human down the road had fallen and needed help. The old woman at the door questioned the use of the word "human," but when she saw the worry in the young man's eyes, she called for help. The ambulance came and took the woman to the hospital, where she was treated and released.

The old neighbor woman came by her cottage the next morning to ask how she was doing. "Thank goodness your brother was visiting," said the neighbor.

"My brother?" the woman asked.

"Yes, he was your brother, wasn't he? Why, you and he have the exact same color hair. Quite unique," she smiled.

The young woman looked out her kitchen window and peered across her garden to the heathered fields beyond. A family of foxes stood, ears erect, eyes staring straight at her.

"Yes, quite unique," she answered. "My family is quite unique," she added, pulling her shining, red locks into a long ponytail on top of her head. "Thanks for stopping by," she called out as the neighbor crossed the garden and walked through the front gate.

❧ Sirens' Song ❧

O nce upon a time, in a land of fae and sea monsters, certain women with healing powers were considered evil. Lucky to escape burning, some of these women were taken on ships and banished to desolate islands of the sea.

On one such voyage, groups of wise women were chained and thrown into dark caverns in the hull. These women all had pets—some cats, some ravens, some foxes— but they set the animals free in the woodlands when they knew their captors were coming. All except their little mice, that is. These friends would not abandon them to this plight.

Mice were hated as much as these women were, but the women and their rodents became loving companions. Each grew to understand the words and squeaks of the other, and each felt a kinship with those who were also maligned.

The mice hid inside the hems of the women's long skirts and, in doing so, became captives at sea, as well. The sailors did not see them at first, but as days continued on, some mice were spied stealing crumbs of bread from the cook's galley.

The sailors despised these beings, calling them vermin and disease harbingers. At every chance, they would try to kill one of them. Sometimes, they succeeded, breaking the women's hearts.

Each night, the mice would squeak gently in the darkness and sing to the women, easing their sorrow. Each morning, they would climb onto their shoulders and gently kiss the dirty faces where tears had left smudged trails the night before. The women were given just enough food to survive, but they always shared with those they loved.

The voyage to these islands of banishment was treacherous. High, rocky cliffs lined the fog-laden coast, and ships would often meet a deadly fate. One night, a horrendous wind howled above the hull. The boat rocked with fury, and the tiny mice shivered in fear.

The women knew their fate; they had ways of seeing what would come the next morning, before the moon had hidden in the daylight sky. Rowboats descended from the ship, but not for them. Holding bony hands, they said a prayer of love. The strongest magic comes from love, not evil. It was a pity that men did not realize this. They said some words and gathered all their friends into a tiny circle.

Suddenly, the long tails of the mice turned into silky fins. Behind their huge ears, delicate gills formed. Their fur changed into glittering scales. Their squeaky voices changed into melodic song.

"Be free, little loves," the women cried.

The ship filled with water. The women held each other tightly as they met their fate.

The little mice were carried on the waves to the depths of the sea, where they began to sing. Sailors in the rowboats atop the waves listened to the magic, such beauty their ears had never heard before.

They sang and they sang, until every sailor was plunged into the depths. And their voices echo to this day. Their siren songs tempt sailors, kin to those who killed their friends. They lure the sailors to the depths of the sea in storms and fogs, forever, to join the ones they loved.

ꕥ Formed from Tears ꕥ

O nce upon a time, in a desolate land by the sea, lived a cruel farmer and his wife. She was young and kind and had married the farmer to escape the hurts her young life had already garnered. But the man was not all he had seemed, and only more hurt continued behind the closed doors of her marriage.

Soon, the wife was with child and traveled to her sister's land, many miles away, to give birth. The birth was not an easy one, and she had to stay in bed for several months. This angered the man, who wanted his wife and child to journey home immediately.

In revenge, the man sold the woman's two cats to the village butcher. Only when she returned to an empty cottage did the woman learn their fate, and her cruel husband laughed. She cried and pleaded to know where they were, but he laughed. Finally, he told her, and her heart broke in two.

In those times, there was no way out of a cruel marriage. The woman remained, her child grew, and soon, she had more children. They eased the break in her heart, but it was always there.

She never brought another animal to her cottage, but she fed all the wild ones in the woods. She fed them every day, with whatever scraps she could save and whatever meager money she could hide away by sewing and knitting for the village women of wealth. She could not save those she had loved, but she could save the rest. And she loved them all—the mangiest, the lamest, the most disfigured. All were held close in her heart.

Years passed, and the woman grew old, grey strands replacing her once raven locks. Her husband grew old and feeble, as well. They lived together in the small cottage, but they lived apart; there was no love any longer, and each day, the woman's heart grew a little blacker with sorrow. Her children were grown and lived in villages far away, with children of their own. Her only joys in life were the wild cats and dogs and foxes and birds and woodland beings that came to her feet each day in love and trust. Now, there was no dream of escape any longer, except in death.

When her time grew near, the woman decided she would not be buried in the pauper plot that surely awaited her and her spouse. He could lie among the weeds; she would not be by his side. One morning, she wrapped herself in her softest knitted shawl and walked out into the woodland to meet her family. Yes, they were her family. She talked to them, and she knew what they were thinking in return.

• • •

The animals knew she was dying; they could sense when time was near. And so they began to make her a beautiful burial mound in the woods. The squirrels carried branches in their mouths. The crows carried straw from nearby barns. The foxes built up the earth and leaves, and the dogs and cats helped create the mound with their paws. The porcupines lay brambles and briars on top. The hedgehogs chewed the last of the autumn roses and spread them across the mound. It was a beautiful mound, fit for a queen.

The beavers created a beautiful log coffin, which the deer pulled with wisteria vines to the burial mound. The woman took her last breath with all those she loved around her. They licked her face and hands and stayed by her side until she closed her eyes for the last time. Then, holding on to her clothing with their teeth, all the strongest of wild wolves lifted her into the log coffin. The animals sealed the mound with dirt.

Snow came soon after, and snow after snow after snow followed. The briar and brambles took root and wound around the entire mound. And her burial site remained a secret for generation after generation.

In time, all her woodland friends had perished, but her legend was told and retold to all their children and children's children to follow. Her mound was never disturbed.

One day, two men came upon the mound in the woods. Some crows watched from the trees as they started poking and digging at her burial site. They listened, because crows are very smart and understand language.

"This looks very promising and untouched," one of the men said.

"Ouch!" yelled the other, his hand bleeding from a briar thorn. "We will never get through this thicket without the right tools. Let's come back tomorrow with the team and start excavating."

Now, the crows didn't exactly know what excavating meant, but they were smart enough to surmise that it wasn't a good thing. They flew throughout the woodlands, telling all the animals the peril that awaited their legendary shrine. The ravens and hawks joined in, and soon, all the woodland was aware of the alarm.

Scores of animals gathered that night and decided to open the mound and hide the honored body. The wolves and dogs and cats began digging beside the foxes. The squirrels and crows and ravens carried away branches, and the beavers chewed through the logs, which were old and decayed and easy to chew after all this time.

They opened the coffin. All had decayed into dust....except for one thing. The woman's heart, so deluged with sorrow, had turned into a large, white pearl. All the sadness of hundreds of teardrops formed this jewel within the shell of her blackened heart. The animals gazed in wonder at the lustrous orb of light, shining in the moonlight.

A large, grey cat stepped forward and picked up the pearl in his paws. "I am taking this to the sea," he said, and he carried the pearl as all the other animals followed. At the edge of a sea cliff, the cat let the pearl descend into the waves. Then, the animals returned to the woods and mounded back the soil.

In the morning, the two men returned with a crew of workmen. They toiled for hours and finally came upon a pile of decaying wood and dust.

"Nothing of value here," one sighed in disgust.

✎ Rusty and Ruby ✎

I will end this book with a real life fairy tale. Once upon a time, a woman was looking for a little dog to fill the empty spot her toy poodle, Poppy, had left inside her heart and home.

Then, one day on social media, this woman read about a rescuer in New York who arranged flights from Shanghai, China to JFK Airport, NY to save dogs from being killed in the meat trade. The rescuer lived about 30 minutes away from one of the woman's grandchildren. So, one December day, after her grandson's birthday party, the woman arranged to visit the rescuer's home to see a tiny, female chocolate poodle named Ruby. Renamed, that is, for her Chinese name was Arya.

Arya was a breeding dog in Shanghai. Breeding dogs remain of "worth" for about five years; after that, their optimum breeding years are behind them. They are kept in cages, filthy and matted, without human love and affection. Arya, being five years old, was sold to a meat truck in Shanghai. She was literally rescued off the truck as it headed for the meat market.

Arya's photo was on the rescuer's social media page, along with a description bearing the word "gentle." The woman just happened upon it—not a coincidence in this magical universe of ours. When this woman got to the rescuer's home, Arya was very, very shy. She had been through so much trauma that greeting humans was not easy for her.

Suddenly, this little bundle of energy flew into the room and landed belly up at the woman's feet. "I think he made his choice," the rescuer said.

His name was Ming-Ming, and he had only been in the US for one day, having landed at JFK the night before. Ming-Ming was found wandering the streets of Shanghai. They were able to locate his owner, who did not want him because he was in need of surgery. Pets less than perfect in China are disregarded in this manner. A tiny thing like Ming-Ming would not last long on the street; there are those looking to kidnap dogs for the meat trade. Somehow, Ming-Ming eluded capture. He was rescued by a kind Chinese teacher who paid for his surgery and helped make it possible for the American rescuers to bring him to New York. She fell in love with him, but her mother-in-law in Shanghai did not permit her to keep him. So, Ming-Ming boarded a flight to NY. He was renamed Rusty because of the color of his fur.

The woman knew Rusty *wanted* her for his mom, but she also knew Ruby *needed* a mom to love her. So, she took the two of them home. When they arrived, Rusty and Ruby jumped onto the couch as if they had lived there all their lives. The woman's Irish wolfhound and collie accepted the new arrivals into their pack, and the rest is history.

Rusty seems no worse for wear from his wandering days in Shanghai. Veterinarians disagree on his age; one has him at about the same age as Ruby, while another believes he is quite an old gent. No matter, he is a pampered baby now.

Ruby has blossomed into a gentle girl, but sometimes, loud noises make her flinch. One can only guess the horrors she endured in that filthy cage.

One more thing...the teacher, now retired in China, and the woman have become friends. The woman calls her Rusty and Ruby's Chinese mom, since she rescued them both. And, an even more miraculous thing happened. The woman sent copies of her fairy tales to Shanghai, and Chinese students are learning English from her stories. The students sent videos to Rusty and Ruby's American mom to thank her. Through her fairy tales, the woman hopes to spread more compassion toward all beings in the minds and hearts of these young students.

By now, I'm sure you have guessed that I am the woman in the story. It has been over two years since that fateful day, two years I could never have imagined without either one of them in my life. It just goes to show you, not all fairy tales happen in castles. Some happen right in your own living room and in your own heart.